D0010701

Dear Parents:

Congratulations! Your child is taking the first steps on an exciting journey. The destination? Independent reading!

STEP INTO READING® will help your child get there. The program offers five steps to reading success. Each step includes fun stories and colorful art or photographs. In addition to original fiction and books with favorite characters, there are Step into Reading Non-Fiction Readers, Phonics Readers and Boxed Sets, Sticker Readers, and Comic Readers—a complete literacy program with something to interest every child.

Learning to Read, Step by Step!

Ready to Read **Preschool–Kindergarten**
• big type and easy words • rhyme and rhythm • picture clues
For children who know the alphabet and are eager to begin reading.

Reading with Help **Preschool–Grade 1**
• basic vocabulary • short sentences • simple stories
For children who recognize familiar words and sound out new words with help.

Reading on Your Own **Grades 1–3**
• engaging characters • easy-to-follow plots • popular topics
For children who are ready to read on their own.

Reading Paragraphs **Grades 2–3**
• challenging vocabulary • short paragraphs • exciting stories
For newly independent readers who read simple sentences with confidence.

Ready for Chapters **Grades 2–4**
• chapters • longer paragraphs • full-color art
For children who want to take the plunge into chapter books but still like colorful pictures.

STEP INTO READING® is designed to give every child a successful reading experience. The grade levels are only guides; children will progress through the steps at their own speed, developing confidence in their reading.

Remember, a lifetime love of reading starts with a single step!

Published in the United States by Random House Children's Books, a division of Penguin Random House LLC, 1745 Broadway, New York, NY 10019, and in Canada by Penguin Random House Canada Limited, Toronto.

Visit us on the Web!
StepIntoReading.com
rhcbooks.com

Educators and librarians, for a variety of teaching tools, visit us at RHTeachersLibrarians.com

ISBN 978-0-593-57114-9 (trade) — ISBN 978-0-593-57115-6 (lib. bdg.)

Printed in the United States of America
10 9 8 7 6 5 4 3 2 1

STEP 2 READING WITH HELP

STEP INTO READING®

Barbie™

YOU CAN BE A DOCTOR

adapted by Elle Stephens
based on a story by Lisa Rojany
illustrated by Mattel and Jiyoung An

Random House New York

Malibu and Brooklyn want to be doctors. They visit a local doctor's office.

They meet a nurse
named Mira.
Malibu and Brooklyn
are going to help.

A little girl
named Lily
is waiting with
her father.

Lily is nervous.

Her arm is in a cast.

Malibu and Brooklyn

tell her not to worry.

Lily smiles.

Nurse Mira comes
to get the girls.

"See you soon!"
they tell Lily.
The friends follow
Nurse Mira.
They are ready
to help!

Malibu and Brooklyn
wash their hands.
They put on
lab coats.

Malibu helps Nurse Mira
with an exam.
She says hello
to a boy named Oliver.

Nurse Mira checks
Oliver's weight.
Malibu writes it down
on his chart.

Then they check
Oliver's height.
"You are getting tall!"
says Nurse Mira.

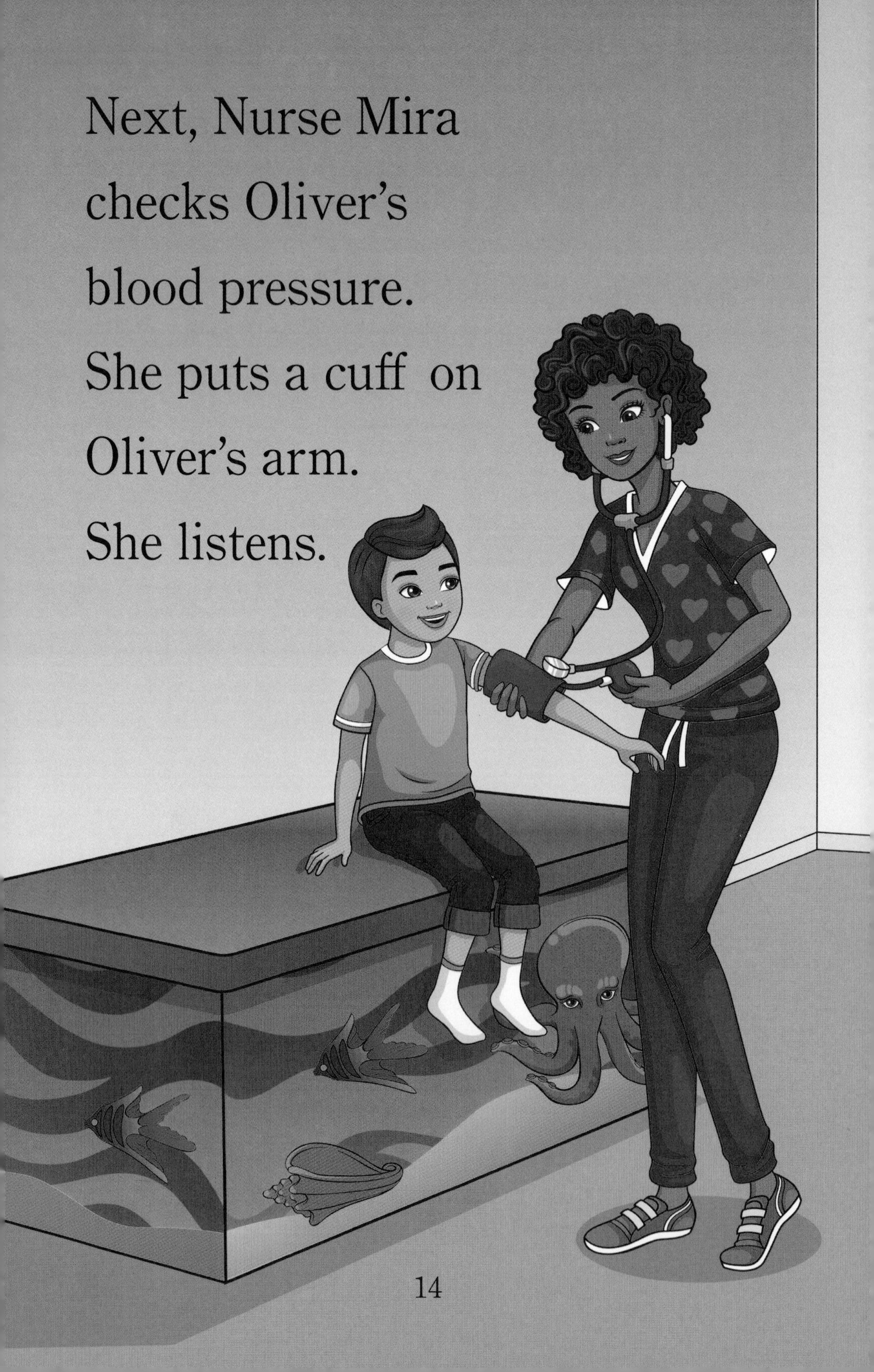

Next, Nurse Mira
checks Oliver's
blood pressure.
She puts a cuff on
Oliver's arm.
She listens.

It is good.
Malibu writes it
on his chart.

Just then,
Dr. Vargas comes in.
She is ready
to see Oliver.

Dr. Vargas starts
Oliver's exam.
She uses a special tool
to check his ears.

Then the doctor asks Oliver questions. They talk about exercise and eating healthy.

Malibu listens
with Oliver's mom.
She is learning
so much!

Brooklyn follows
Dr. Vargas
to another exam.

They check the chart
on the door.
Lily is the next patient!

Lily is ready
to get her cast off.

First, Dr. Vargas wants to make sure Lily's arm is healed.

Brooklyn takes Lily
to the X-ray room.
The X-ray will take
a picture of Lily's bone.
An X-ray tech
takes the X-rays.

“Great job!”

Brooklyn tells Lily.

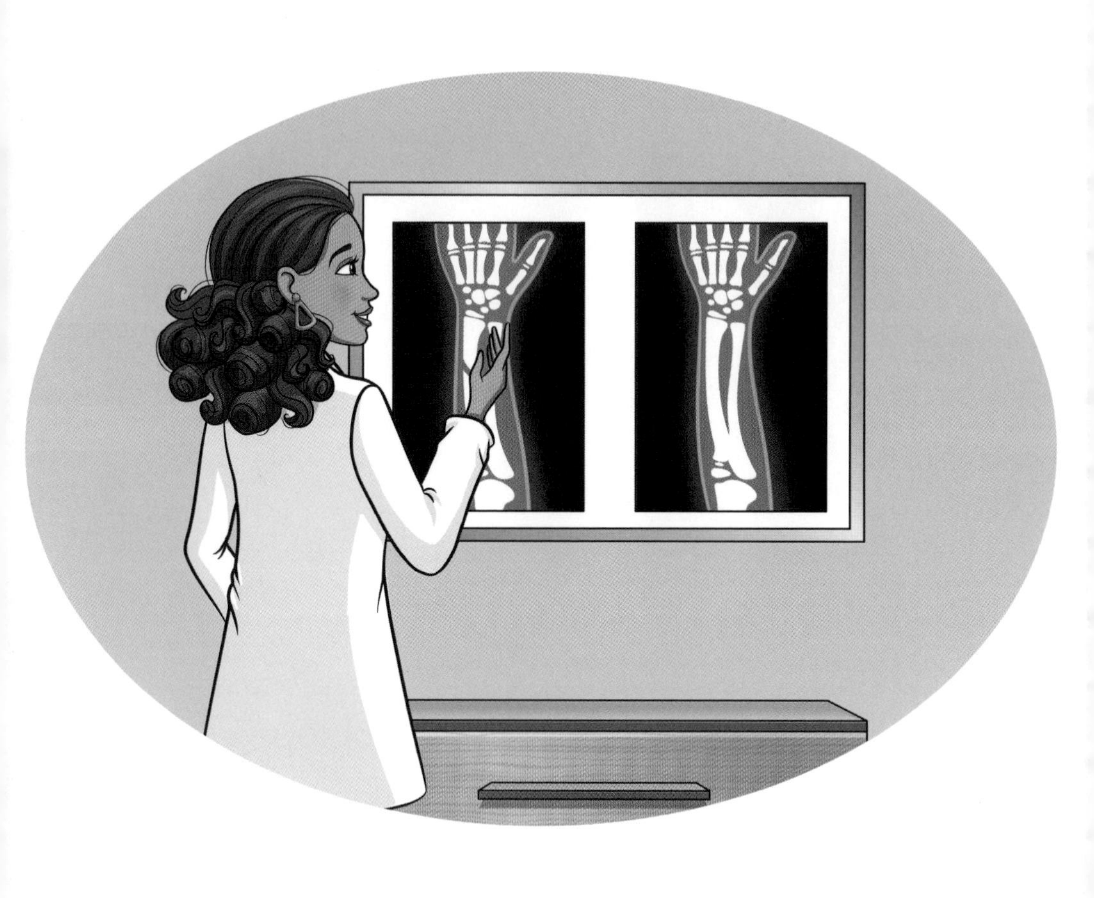

Dr. Vargas looks
at the X-rays.
Lily's bone is
all better!

"Good news," says Brooklyn.
"We can take
your cast off!"

Dr. Vargas cuts the cast
with a special saw.
Then she uses a tool
to open it up.

Brooklyn helps take
off the cast.
Lily bends her arm
and wiggles her fingers.

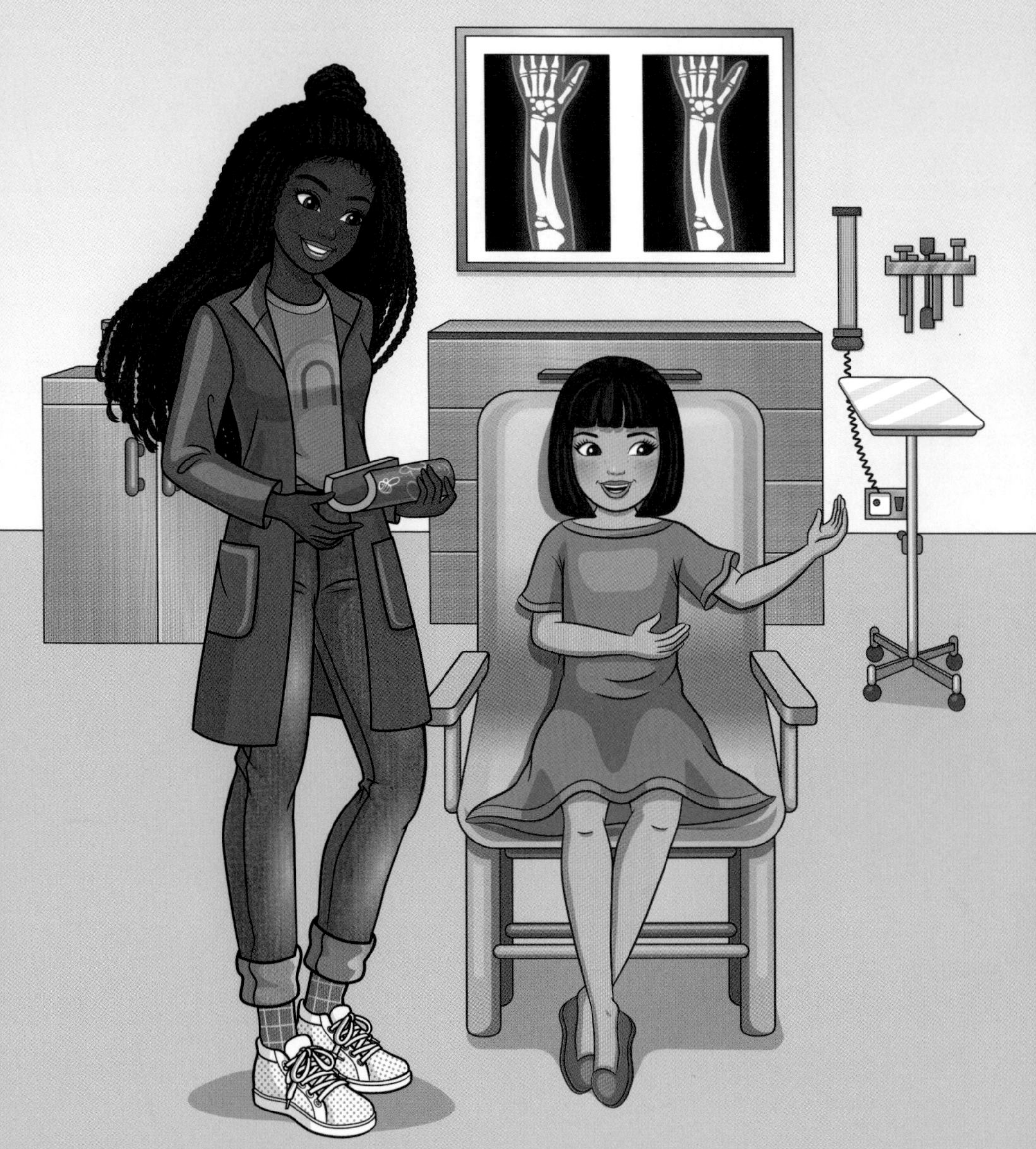

Lily asks Brooklyn
and Malibu to sign her cast.

The friends help Lily
pick a special prize.
Lily chooses a
purple bouncy ball.

Malibu and Brooklyn love
helping Dr. Vargas.
"You can be a
doctor, too!"
says Dr. Vargas.